# THE HOME OF THE WORLD

# THE HOME
# OF THE WORLD

# DEJAN STOJANOVIĆ

New Avenue Books

# NOTE TO THIS EDITION

The poems in this collection are part of a series titled *The Embrace of Light and Darkness,* marking their first publication in book form. The collection includes poems originally written in English between 2005 and 2010, with a few exceptions added or fixed later.

*D. S.*

# Contents

# SONGS OF LIGHT

# SONG OF LIGHT

The grass is less green now,
Air is less fresh, and even the blue is less blue.

I don't go to the shore anymore
To watch the sea embrace the light,

To ask the Sun a new question.
I'm losing an old friend;

He used to tell me stories
In gentle whispers through the light.

"Sun, shine upon him," I heard a voice in the air,
"He is blind without you and feels lost;

Give him back his sight,
Grant him fresh air and restored senses;

Let him see, hear, smell, feel, and breathe;
Give him back his wings and let him fly toward you again."

## SONG IN THE GARDEN

Come to my secret Oasis, she said,
To see my flowers,
To listen to my birds.
Come to my Oasis

To admire my fountains,
To see the sounds and hear the light,
To experience my uniquely mixed world,
To inhale the colors and fragrances,

And tell me what you feel
When you see the light in my eyes,
When you listen to the silent sounds.
Come to my Oasis, she said.

# SONG OF ELYSIUM

On the bridges, in the parks and gardens,
In the places where we don't expect it, bliss happens,

Sinking into silence,
We attune ourselves to the secret language,

By recognizing each other
In every song and face, every scent and sound.

We listen to the trembling beat in our chests.
It never lies.

We listen as our senses awaken and sharpen.
They never lie.

We see the Elysium,
And we slowly walk in.

# A SONG WITHIN A SONG

We traveled a long way and forgot
The reason for the invention of poetry.
It is a prayer, a sacrifice,
And a means of purification.

Poetry served to attract rain,
To invoke the presence of God,
Or to seek guidance
On unpromising, gloomy mornings.

It is a miracle, a magical sound,
It is a remedy and a soothing balm.

# THE DREAM SONG

Sing with your full voice
And let your melody grow within me;

Then fly down until you reach the bottom,
Searching to find me;

Wake me with your song,
Then, soar back to the heights,

Sing from your distant heights,
Wave to me and show me the way;

Look for me everywhere,
And share what you uncover while searching;

Sing with your full voice,
And travel through the world to find me;

I have been waiting for you in storms,
Waiting for you in sadness,

And in dreams, for
You were my destination;

Dream for me and sing,

For I have been asleep for so long;

Come to my dreams to find me,

So we can dream awake and together.

Awaken me from awakeness

So I can dream an absolute dream.

# AWAKENING

# GOD

I see your science—
A simple discovery—
You are me, and I am you.

Words, words, words;
Too many words
Obstruct the way

To simple discoveries.

# ETERNAL FATHER

Come closer, distant creature;
Let me see your face.
Come closer, even if your light
Or darkness may destroy me.

It is not a fair game,
Following wrong steps
Into the dead ends
Of an endless labyrinth.

Come closer, wild Spirit,
Even as a chimera or mirage;
Let me see your face,
My dearest friend and father.

# AWAKENING

Why deceive
Flying into new territories
Without being ready?

Why dream
Without understanding
New revelations?

Why know
Without feeling
The simple joy of awakening?

Why wake
Without burning?

## CURE

With every revelation,

We believed we had discovered the truth

Beyond mere words,

Finding solace only

In phrases that had the power

To heal our souls.

# PRETENSE

Why all the noise,
All that pretense?
Talks of glory—if

Beyond words and fame,
There lives a simple world,
Equally generous to all.

# SOUL OF THE UNKNOWN

Who are you?
Eternity asks.

I am the wave of the soul
And the soul of the wave.

Of what? Eternity asks.
Of the unknown, Darkness replied.

# THE EAGLE AND THE FATA MORGANA

# I WAS AN EAGLE

In my dream, I was an eagle soaring,
Accompanied by soft clouds.
I watched them flee, disappearing,
Finding a new home for life.
In my dream, I was a dream.

A whisper echoed through the void,
Moving swiftly through space.
I was that whisper, dreaming the dreamer's dream.
His magic force kept me dreaming;
In his dream, I am a dream.

# SECRET KNOWLEDGE

I never know where my knowledge comes from,

Or what purpose it serves.

If only I could understand the true reason,

I could endure more easily

As I seek to discover and reveal

The secret, whose distant flame I sense.

# OTHER PLACES

Tell me about other places,
The driving force of the Universe,
Holding more to explore than dreams
That blind us, turning thoughts into verse.

Tell me of other senses,
Other dimensions that remain unseen:
Beyond death, there is more awaiting us,
More than we could ever agree on.

# AN ORDINARY DAY

Everything felt ordinary:

People walked along crowded streets,

Women flaunted their tanned legs,

Casual glances drew attention

From both lazy men and those in a hurry.

Children played in the yards,

Yelling and scoring in their games.

It was just an ordinary day filled with small rewards.

On the beach, basking in the sunshine,

The noise grew louder

From people playing volleyball,

Earning applause here and there,

In a day that revealed little

About how important it all truly was.

## PARKS AND STREETS

As he walks down the street, he thinks of another—
Perhaps one in Florence, Paris, or New York.
He reflects on the beauty yet to be discovered
And continues to walk, dream, and think.

Parks embody a universal quality;
They are tranquil oases
Separated from their noisy surroundings,
Like heaven in a human jungle.
Although cities differ greatly,
All parks share a similar essence.

In one park, he experienced the love
He had lost in another.
To get from one park to another,
He had to traverse various streets.
These streets lay in different time zones,
Yet all the parks existed in the same temporal space.

He began to feel diminished
And started moving faster through the streets,
Which began to blend into a single avenue.
It was not the Champs-Élysées or Boulevard Saint-Michel,

Nor was it Park Avenue or Fifth Avenue.

It was not Michigan Avenue in Chicago,

Avenida 9 de Julio in Buenos Aires,

Piazza del Popolo or Piazza Venezia in Rome,

Palazzo della Signoria in Florence,

Campo dei Santi Giovanni e Paolo in Venice,

Corso Vittorio Emanuele II in Milan,

Parliament Street in Exeter, England,

Prince Michael Street in Belgrade,

Or Red Square in Moscow.


It was all the avenues combined

Leading toward the park, he discovered

While he wasn't actively looking for it

As he walked down a street, he thought he did not like.

Strange thoughts revived in unfamiliar lands.

# ROSEBUD IN A FAIRY TALE

## ROSEBUD

Don't say a word;
A rose blooms in silence.

Protect it from the wind,
From the crowd and the noise.

Only let the light in
And allow the ground to do its work.

Wait patiently
Until you see the Rosebud.

# UNCERTAINTY

He was heading in the wrong direction,
Unaware of it.

It was too late to turn back,
And staying put seemed like the better option.

Not long after, he noticed
Many people were going the same way.

Curious, he asked why they were taking this route.
They replied, "To escape."

"From what?" he wondered.
"From boredom and uncertainty," they said.

# TEMPLE OF HOPE

We declare: We are the ones
Who will build the Temple of Hope,
To remember that the sky is blue,
To listen to the whispers of the ocean,
And to find joy in the wonders of life.

You say:
You will not change anything;
The world will remain the same.
It is what it is.

Yet, there is still hope
That this will not just be a war of words.

## DEEDS

Her deeds had wings;

They soared and took on a life of their own.

Rewarded with laughter and wisdom,

Encouraged and healed,

She developed her own wings,

Flying toward the land

Of hidden wisdom and knowledge.

And she never spoke of it.

# VICTORY

Victories need no explanations.

Winners understand there is no true winning;

They do what must be done.


True victories are felt rather than announced.

Trophies cannot measure genuine victories.

Wisdom is the ultimate triumph


If true wisdom is even possible

To achieve or recognize.

# NOWHERE

In striving for perfection,

He mastered the art of anonymity,

Became imperceptible

And arrived from nowhere to nowhere.

## EARLY RETIREMENT

He was a well-behaved child.

Many saw him as a born philosopher.

He had answers to nearly everything

And retired at an early age.

# VANITY

How many stories would remain unwritten
Or inventions never created?

How many battles would not have been won?
How many temples would not have been built?

How many women would be less happy,
And how many would be much happier?

How many songs would go unheard,
While quarrels could have been avoided?

How much more stable would we be,
And how much closer to one another,

Without vanity?

## TOO LATE

They spoke of eternity,
But their actions were temporary.

They spoke of wisdom,
Yet their actions were damaging.

They spoke of brotherhood,
And the outcome was division.

And now,
It's too late.

## YOU KNOW IT, YOU FEEL IT

What are you searching for—
Do you know?
What are you longing for—
Do you feel?

What makes you feel this—
Do you know?
What makes you know this—
Do you feel?

You know it by feeling;
You feel it by knowing.

# MEANING

I cannot teach you anything, the teacher said.

Just open your eyes.

# MY OTHER SELF

I am a slave to desire,
I am a slave to pride,
I am a slave to vice,
I am a slave to success.

"Get rid of desire," Desire said.
"Get rid of pride," Pride said.
"Get rid of vices," Honor said.
"Get rid of competition," Success said.

I will still be a slave to sin,
A slave to materialism,
A slave to love,
A slave to myself.

"Get rid of sin and lust,
Of materialism and love,
And you will get rid of yourself,"
Said my other self.

"Are you proposing suicide?" I asked sadly.
"No, I would never suggest that," my other self replied.
"Then what are you trying to say?"
"Just be yourself," said my other self.

# POETS

# WALT WHITMAN

Captain, our captain,

We take your hand,

Following in your footsteps on the streets

Of Chicago, New York, and San Francisco.

Your spirit rises from the grassy fields,

Appearing on the horizon

As a beam of light signaling to America,

Reminding her of her roots.

We follow a trail of light.

Leading to forgotten springs,

Placing our ears on the ground

To get closer to the leaves of grass and listen

With a desire to understand transformed America.

# A LETTER TO EMILY DICKINSON

A word thrown into silence

Always finds its echo somewhere,

Where silence opens hidden lexicons,

And words return to silence,

Arriving at just the right moment.

# WILLIAM BUTLER YEATS

To achieve the simplicity

Of words that have learned to dance

Without much support from a dancer

Who mastered the steps of a worthy life

From those who excelled in the art of dance.

Is it a dance or the act of dancing?

Is it to live or to be lived?

It is not the dancer but the dance;

It is not life but the living mind,

The truth of existence found in dance.

If he had chosen only to live,

The dance would have been much less lively.

A great dancer follows the steps

Only life knows how to choreograph.

# ROBERT FROST

At the crossroads, there is a word
That signifies the open road ahead.
A song is rising from the dark woods
Of expanding, equally perilous cities.

A vast family rides on horses,
Traveling along different paths,
Exploring and discovering why
One road is better than another.

A word sent to open the road
Transforms that road into a melodic path;
The road chooses the rider,
And the song becomes the journey.

A word that opens the road
Allows the road to sing the rider's song.

# WALLACE STEVENS

The sea was a house, and the world was a ship.
You were both the sea and the ship.

The ship was stormy, while the sea was calm,
And the house waited for the world

To arrive by way of the ship on the sea.
The sea was a ship, and the world was a house.

You were the ship in the sea—
The house and the world.

The world was the ship in the sea,
And the sea was inside the house.

# THE UNUSUAL LOVE SONG OF T. S. ELIOT

At twenty-six, I was inexperienced;

Still, I knew a lot about love

In the wasteland of reasoning.

It's not important when you start

Practicing, but rather when you begin searching.

I committed myself to finding love

Before others even knew it existed, *breeding*

*Lilacs out of the dead land, mixing*

My thoughts, my longings, my love

For something that didn't need naming.

In the misty mornings, I recognized

The dew on the petals, alive yet sleepy.

I was a dreamer, I admit, thinking,

*April is the cruelest month*, flying

Thoughts about some distant teaching,

Seeing the invisible in the visible, loving

Wild ideas that make love, searching

To find it; love was a secret hard to decode—

Sacred to me, it was. Students talked

Of business, Dante, and Michelangelo;

That was important, yet not so vital

In the land where death died long ago, blooming

Roses taught me a lesson, awakening

The land where human measures are important

Yet not so crucial, so I stayed, deserving

A degree from real roses, forgetting

The Ph.D. that was waiting for me at Harvard.


Yet, it was not about Michelangelo,

But does it matter? I saw paintings

And landscapes—both dead lands and alive ones—

Understanding that feeling is more important than knowing.

I had everything in my head,

And I remained in a place where dreaming

Was more important than competing


In the land where women come and go, talking

Of Sarah Bernhardt and Coco Chanel in the Sistine Chapel,

And men come and go, talking

About wars. Children come and go, talking

Of chocolate, and they all go, leaving

Not much to ponder when exchanging

Experiences with feelings, transforming


Experiences into meanings, mixing

Thoughts about love evaporating

Into "the yellow fog that rubs its back upon the window panes,
The yellow smoke that rubs its muzzle on the window panes;"
And in the end, I understood April, learning
That April seemed cruel only in the dead land, knowing
That every month is equally paradisiacal and hellish,
Equally paradoxical.

## e. e. cummings

there may be greater poets, perhaps
but there is only one cummings.

*to be nobody but yourself*
is indeed the hardest fight.

Plato did not say this
or we wouldn't believe it.

he heard us in the silence
unknowingly, we spoke to him, and

he sent us an old word
flying over the new yet unnamed avenue.

we heard him whispering
Avenue of Love,

and we promised, under his spell of love,
to never tell.

# THE WAY

# THE WAY

The tree—
Growing from nowhere
Into nowhere

Between nowhere
And nowhere—
The Way

# THE WAY AND THE TRUTH

In the beginning,
There was an overwhelming loneliness.

Truth took the first step
And began to listen to its own footsteps.

That's how the conversation started,
Making loneliness more bearable.

As Truth moved further
The path became brighter.

Then, Truth began to listen
To how the Way communicates.

The Way became the only path,
The sole purpose of Truth.

As a result, the Truth and the Way
Became one and the same.

# BEING AND NOTHING

Time and space are void;
This should be obvious.

Nothing is simply nothing,
Which means it is void.

If Being lacks space,
Then it, too, must be nothing.

Time, space, and nothing
Are all the same.

If time, space, and nothing are indeed nothing,
Then, nothing can be new.

There is no concept of old and new
In nothing.

Everything must be both
Old and new at the same time.

If there is no space and no time,
Where are we, and where are we going?

Is Being hidden within space?
Or does space exist within Being?

Who is fighting against whom?
Who is stronger?

Does Being enter space,
Or does space enter Being?

# THE WAY BACK

From the Darkness I came,
Traveling a long way.

I am here now
To stay for a while,
But then I must find the way back.

# SHELL

I am the largest and the smallest—
The shell of the Universe.

# BLACK STARS

## BEFORE AND AFTER

Before the first before
And after the last after
There is night waiting,

Almost nonexistent
Yet so constant
Night in the Heart of Light.

## IN THE HEART OF THE NIGHT

Before it was born
The day was darker than the night.
It held the whole Darkness

Within itself,
And from its dark Heart
The Light shone.

# THE NIGHT IS ALWAYS AWAKE

When the whole world is sleeping,
The night remains awake, faithfully waiting.

There is nothing more faithful than the night.
Nothing can escape its eternal love.

# ETERNITY

Black stars in black waters.
Black emptiness
Swallowed by black Light.

White Light emerges
From the black stars
In the black sea.

White swallows black;
Then, black swallows white
For all eternity.

# FAIRY TALE

Shining dots in the sky—
White holes in the black sea—
Doors to an old home,

A distant place—
Enlightened joy
Eternal bliss.

With lost reality,
Distant, yet present, desire
Craves to merge.

# HOME

There is only one home,
Only one story to tell,
Only One Way
To one destination.

There is only one Harbor,
Only one shining Heart,
Where all the suns are born.

That is our Home.

# THE HOME OF THE WORLD

# ONE WORLD—ONE HOME—ONE MIND

Stormy oceans give birth to the Light.
Nights are remnants of that Light,
Leftovers of darkness as the world is born
From a hellish kiss of Darkness and Light.

Life is a destination,
The reason to fall and rise,
The reason to reinvent the same,
The world within the world.

Death is as necessary as life,
Darkness is needed to see the Light,
Tears are not the enemies of smiles;
The only path is connection.

We live in death and die in life,
May see in darkness and be blinded by light.
We laugh and cry together,
Through this day and this night.

# THE SPIRIT OF THE WORLD

## I

The world is my embrace of the unknown,
A fusion of my spirit, soul, and essence—
My enduring hope.

The world is my cherished companion,
Filled with love and challenges—
The journey of my life.

The world is my Infinite Ocean and tranquil Island,
The guiding lighthouse—
My blooming rose.

The world flows through my veins,
With stars as its blood cells—
It is my only chance.

The world reflects my vision, holds my memories,
Captures your essence—
It grants me wings to soar.

The world is my flourishing garden,
Rich with diverse flora and fauna—
It is my Kingdom of Growth.

The world is my source of harmony, a book waiting to be
    unlocked,
A whisper eager to be heard—
It is my paradise.

The world embodies my fire, stirring passions and desires,
Fuelling my will to thrive—
It tests my resilience.

The world represents my struggle for rebirth,
Bridging endings and new beginnings—
It is my purgatory of transformation.

The world nourishes my breath,
Offering salvation even in solitude—
It is my precious time.

The world is my light bulb, casting brilliance into space,
Embodying love and illuminating the path to life—
It is my Masterpiece.

The world invites me to walk into the night,
To seek the light and share my journey—
It is my Way.

The world blossoms with an array of colors,

A garden of red, white, yellow, and black roses shimmering in
     darkness—

It is my home of stars.


The world is my home and a lighthouse of hope for all.

## II

Spirit of the Universe awakens with the thunder,
Measured by the sound of light,
It embodies its children in the world;
They are its life.

Omnipresent emptiness,
Lonely space in waiting;
Its atoms and galaxies
Are whispers in the night.

As it travels through itself,
Its waves crash against the dual shores
Of loneliness, falling
Into empty necessity.

It gives birth to space
By inhaling and exhaling.
Its only desire
Is to live and never die.

Its love is life;
Its life is love:
Two truths from the same dream;
Darkness is merely the other side.

It sets in motion
A multitude from oneness,
A majestic competition
Of life in movement.

It allows them to fight
To create order;
It permits them to consume each other
To maintain it.

It is the thunder;
They are its light.
There is no evil,
Except for the cost of motion.

It makes the oceans
And creates the shores.
It is the darkness
Born of light.

It is old—
Older than darkness,
Older than light,
Darker than night.

It is the light,
Older than light.
We pay the price
For Its delight.

It disrupts the peace of nothingness,
The harmony of emptiness;
It thunders and bursts into the night.
All creation is almost diabolical.

Galaxies are the treetops of the invisible Universe.
There is no birth of anything
Without a pain,
There is no beauty without a price.

It is the Father, the Mother, and the Son.
There is no evil;
The devil is merely
The other face of God.

## III

There is no outside,
No time or space beyond the Spirit of the Universe.
It is both the beginning and the end,
Yet, there is truly no beginning or end.

Only Its whispers,
Only the essence of Its desires.
There are no enemies, no colonies,
No emperors, no slaves.

Its thunder and Light
Are Its sight and hearing.
Its children are Its life.
It allows some to die so that others may live.

There is no hate
In the wars among Its children,
Only Its will and love
And their desire to survive.

There is no annihilation,
Only the formation
Of Its archipelago in an empty sea,
Its Island of multitude.

He nourishes Itself
By drawing space into Its core,
Growing not outward
But inward.

From Its thunders
Even Nothing is stirred;
From Its Light, Darkness hides;
From Its love, life is born.

Its love reflects It
Because It is love,
And Its love is formidable.
That is the price of life.

It soars and grows,
Moves back and forth.
It seeks to remember
And find Its way back.

There is no rebellion in Its dominion;
It is the only rebel.
There is no Lucifer
Or fallen angel.

It is the Bearer of Light;
It is the sole rebel.
It stole fire
From the selfish night.

It rebels against Darkness,
It disrupts her peace.
It is the fallen angel,
The very source of life.

It is Its creation.
It is the Creator of fire,
Of thunder, mist, and dust,
Of energy and elements.

It creates dragons and black holes.
It creates dark matter,
It creates circles and centrifuges.
Its truth can be Its deceit.

It creates blue skies,
Fresh air, and beauty.
Its beauty is as vast
As Its secrets, swimming in the night.

Its thunders are its revivals;

Its bursts are Its blood.

It flows through your veins;

It nourishes Itself on your journey.


It is both truth and lie;

It is the face never shown.

It rebels against the night.

Its Son shines upon It.


People call Its Son the devil,

But Spirit is reborn in multitude.

It is the Light you crave;

It is a life borne of love.


There is no devil, only the Spirit.

There is no duality, only unity.

The devil was born from weakness,

Not from the dream.


There is no thunder beyond love;

There is no hate in Light.

There is no motion without a price,

And the devil is Its own sacrifice.


There is only the Spirit

That shines upon the world and Itself.

There is only the Spirit whispering your Light
And our eyes and ears.

There is only the Spirit,
That sings in the night,
Only the Spirit
That loves to live and lives to love.

There is only the Spirit,
That never dies and always dreams
Of faith and salvation,
Of reasons to wake up and persist.

Its thunder is Its whisper;
Its life is the Light.
It is the only Father,
The Mother, and the Son.

Your translucent touch,
Its outstretched fingers,
Its omnipresent eye,
Its formidable force—tender and alive.

It is Its dream,
And Its dream dreams Itself.
It is the dream born from a dream,

And It lives Its dream.

It is the Creator;
It makes the world,
It dreams the world,
The world is Its dream.

It lives in dying;
It dies in living.
It is life and death;
It dies only to be reborn.

There is no death,
Only a moment of rest.
There is no end, only a new beginning.
The world never truly dies.

# IV

When the Spirit embraces the darkness,
The darkness shines upon It.
When nights are not truly nights,
Loneliness is not loneliness.

When tomorrow is the same as yesterday,
Yesterday becomes tomorrow.
When tomorrow is merely a past dream,
Yesterday will be reborn.

When darkness longs for light,
Time comes into existence.
When time is compressed,
The world stands still.

When nights are lonely,
Loneliness feels dark.
When night is both day and night,
Emptiness seeks Spirit's light.

When Spirit creates an illusion,
It opens the Space.
When Space is open,
The Spirit is closer to itself the farther it goes.

When light cries for space,
Time is different here and there.
When space is both open and closed,
Spirit is both far and near.

When Spirit fills the circle,
It escapes from it.
When It circles the circle,
It becomes a circle.

When Spirit empties the circle,
It becomes a divider.
When It circles nothingness,
It deceives the night.

When Spirit takes flight,
It becomes a Composer.
When It circles the center,
Night consumes It.

When the world is born from loneliness,
Night transforms into light.
When the day is long and bright,
Light craves emptiness.

When Spirit unites with the night,
New stars are born.
When Spirit shines upon darkness,
It conquers the night.

When today emerges,
The night surrenders to the Spirit.
When It becomes the Master of the Night,
It is also its Light.

When there is no loneliness,
Everything is light.
When It becomes the light,
The light needs only itself.

When light unites with light,
Stars are born and die.
When It shines upon the light,
Spirit overpowers Itself.

When there is no birth,
Spirit yields to Itself.
When It is a slave to Itself,
It becomes the night of light.

When space cries for light,

Time remains the same everywhere.
When there is only open space,
Spirit is everywhere.

When It does not circle,
It is a wave.
When the center moves,
Everything becomes a code.

When everything is reminiscence,
Spirit is Its memory.
When waves become images,
Remembrance is the light.

When nothing moves,
All is an illusion.
When all is fire,
Fire becomes a dream.

When the dream is light,
Night must also dream.
When night seeks to ignite the fire,
Night becomes the Mother of Light.

When Light is the Father,
There are only two of them.

When the Father impregnates the Mother,
Spirit is both the Father and the Son.

When It is both the Father and the Mother,
The Son embodies both the Mother and the Father.
When nothing is everything,
Everything becomes a dream out of nothing.


(When there is no loneliness, loneliness is lonely.)

# V

The Spirit rules and shines upon the night,
Dividing and uniting—
Devil and God in One,
It both gives and takes.

Born from Its desire,
It conquers Itself and gives birth to space.
It travels through Itself,
It is Its own space-time.

It is the Master conquered by Its Son.
It is Its reason, and It is Its life.
It is Its life, and It is Its dream.
It is the Alpha, and it is the Omega.

# CHILDREN OF HOPE

They dwell within the Spirit,
And the Spirit dwells within them;
They are the thoughts of the Spirit,
And Spirit is their destination.

They are Spirit's blood,
Its floods and hurricanes,
Its nirvana and Its hell—
The voice of a multitude.

The voice of the voiceless,
Of the lost and forgotten,
Of the deaf and silent.
They are Its warriors and saints.

They are both mighty and meek;
They are emperors and beggars.
They possess everything and own nothing;
They are the architects of Its dreams.

They are the Masters, and Spirit is the servant;
It is the slaves who shape the Master.
They serve the Spirit by living Its life;

They are the guardians of Its aspirations.

They are Its hands and eyes,
Its Light and delight,
Its fire and growth—
Explosions that conquer the night.

They are alive and dead,
Awakened and asleep;
They create love and inspire destruction,
They exist within Its mind.

They are Its life and dream,
A prayer and a reason to be,
A joyful voice in the sorrowful night.

# ABOUT THE AUTHOR

Dejan Stojanović (1959) was born in Peć, Kosovo (formerly part of Serbia, Yugoslavia). Although he received a legal education, he has never practiced law. Instead, he became a journalist and foreign correspondent in the early 1990s; however, he is primarily a poet, essayist, philosopher, and businessman.

He has published the following poetry collections:

*Circling (Krugovanje),* Narodna knjiga—Alfa, Belgrade, published in three editions: 1993, 1998, and 2000.
*The Sun Watches Itself (Sunce sebe gleda)*, NIP Književna reč, Belgrade, 1999.
*The Sign and Its Children (Znak i njegova deca), Prosveta, Belgrade, 2000.*
*The Creator (Tvoritelj),* Narodna knjiga, Belgrade, 2000.
*The Shape (Oblik),* Gramatik, Podgorica, 2000.

*The Dance of Time (Ples vremena),* Konras, Belgrade, 2007.

Pentalogy: *The World in Nowherness (Svet u nigdini),* Udruženje književnika Srbije, Belgrade, 2017:
(1) *Ozar (Ozar),*
(2) *The World and God (Svet i Bog),*
(3) *The World in Nowhereness (Svet u nigdini),*
(4) *The World and Humans (Svet i ljudi),*
(5) *The Home of Light (Dom svetlosti).*

*The Hidden Light (Skrivena svetlost),* Čigoja, Belgrade, 2018.
*Primordial Spark (Iskra iskona),* Albatros plus, Belgrade, 2021.
*Centuries and Steps (Vekovi i koraci),* Albatros plus, Belgrade, 2023.

Essays:

*Creator and Creating (Stvaralac i stvaranje),* Albatros plus, Belgrade, 2021.
*The New Man and the New World (Novočovek i novosvet),* Rad, Belgrade, 2022.

Anthology: *Selected Serbian Plays* (*Izabrane srpske drame*), USA, 2016.

A book of his selected interviews, *Conversations* (*Razgovori*), was published in 1999 by NIP Književna reč in Belgrade. The Serbian Heritage Foundation and the Association of Writers of Serbia for Intellectual Engagement awarded the book the Rastko Petrović Prize.

*Collected Poems: 1978-2000* (Pentalogy 1), New Avenue Books, 2025 (Translation from Serbian).

Books written in English:

Philosophy: *Absolute,* New Avenue Books, USA, 2024.

Poetry Series: *The Embrace of Light and Darkness* (Pentalogy 3):
- *Dance of Sounds*, New Avenue Books, 2025
- *The Matter of Matter*, New Avenue Books, 2025
- *The Home of the World*, New Avenue Books, 2025
- *All Women in One*, New Avenue Books, 2025
- *Strange Thoughts* (prose), New Avenue Books, 2025

He lived in Chicago, USA, from 1990 to 2014, and holds citizenship in both Serbia and the United States.

www.ingramcontent.com/pod-product-compliance
Lightning Source LLC
Chambersburg PA
CBHW052013240626
47153CB00008B/2857